PIGS in the MUD
in the Middle of the Rud

BY **Lynn Plourde**

ILLUSTRATED BY

John Schoenherr

Down East

ISBN: 0-89272-719-5

Printed in China

Down East
BOOKS·MAGAZINE·ONLINE
www.downeast.com

Distributed to the trade by National Book Network

Library of Congress Control Number: 2005936444

For Paul
with love and thanks
for never once saying,
"Won't do!"
—L. P.

For Claire
for not stopping
the silliness
—J. S.

It had rained. It had poured.
Now a Model T Ford
was stopped in the rud
by some pigs in the mud.

"Pigs in the rud!"
Grandma said.

Oh no. Won't do.
Gotta shoo. But who?

"I'll shoo. That's who,"
Brother said.

And he shooed.
And he squealed.
And he rutted.
And he reeled.

But the pigs didn't budge.
Not a tiny little smudge.

"Hens in the rud!"
Grandma said.

Oh no. Won't do.
Gotta shoo. But who?

"I'll shoo. That's who,"
Sister said.

And she shooed.
And she clucked.
And she squawked.
And she plucked.

But the hens didn't scatter.
Not a tiny little smatter.

"Sheep in the rud!"
Grandma said.

Oh no. Won't do.
Gotta shoo. But who?

"I'll shoo. That's who,"
Mama said.

And she shooed.
And she jeered.
And she baa-ed.
And she sheared.

But the sheep didn't shuffle.
Not a tiny little shmuffle.

"Bulls in the rud!"
Grandma said.

Oh no. Won't do.
Gotta shoo. But who?

"I'll shoo. That's who,"
Papa said.

And he shooed. And he tussled.
And he snorted. And he rustled.

But the bulls didn't charge.
Not a tiny little smarge.

Pigs, hens, sheep, bulls—all in the rud.
Brother, Sister, Mama, Papa—all in the rud.

Oh no. Won't do.
Gotta shoo. But who?

"OOOOOO-EEE! Up to me,"
Grandma said.

With her hands on her hips,
and a snarl on her lips,

and her dander up,
Grandma yelled, . . .

"TIME FOR SUP!"

Budge, scatter,
shuffle, charge.
Smudge, smatter,
shmuffle, smarge.

All to sup.

At last, empty rud.

But look in the mud.

With her dress all rumpled,
and her bonnet all crumpled,
and muddy, head to toe. . .

Grandma said,
"Time to go!"